THE CASE
OF THE
ISSING
ROT CAKE

**ILLUSTRATED BY
DEBORAH ZEMKE**

Boys and girls, this case is about thieves on Ed's farm. The names have been changed to protect the good guys.

Over 100 animals live on this farm. Most work. Some horse around. Others steal.

That's where I come in. My name is Detective Wilcox. I'm a policemouse.

The boss is Captain Griswold. We're MFIs, Missing Food Investigators. It's our job to investigate cases of missing food.

Whatever the food, whatever the crime, we make the bad guys do the time.

It was 10:00 Monday morning. The captain and I were working the day shift when we got our first call.

Captain Griswold

Detective Wilcox

Chapter 1

Case File #1113: The Missing Carrot Cake

10:00 am, Headquarters

"Wilcox, here. Headquarters."

"Hello, this is Miss Rabbit."

"How can I help you?" I asked.

"My cake is gone!"

"What cake?" I asked.

"The cake I baked for my party tomorrow!"

"Stay calm, ma'am. We'll be right there," I said. "Captain, we've got a Code 12 — a missing cake!"

We grabbed some cheese donuts for the road and rushed to our squad car. We headed north across the farm, past the pigpen and chicken coop, straight to Miss Rabbit's hole.

Traffic was light — only a couple of chickens crossing the road.

The Crime Scene

10:15 am, Home of Miss Rabbit

We parked in front of Miss Rabbit's hole. We didn't see anyone, but we could hear a voice.

"Down here," called Miss Rabbit.

We slid down the rabbit hole and landed in the kitchen. Cake crumbs, carrots, and frosting were EVERYWHERE — on the table, on the floor, and all over Miss Rabbit.

"Detective Wilcox, ma'am, and Captain Griswold, MFIs," I said, flashing my badge. "Can you tell us what happened?" I pulled out my pen and notepad.

Note-taking is essential for any MFI.

"I baked a cake for my party tomorrow," said Miss Rabbit. "And now it's gone!"

"What kind of cake?" I asked.

"A carrot cake with cream cheese frosting."

Hmm. . . I wondered which animals liked carrot cake.

"Where was the cake?" I asked.

"Right here, on the kitchen table. I left it to cool and when I came back, there was a big mess and no cake!" Miss Rabbit sobbed.

The captain handed her a hankie.

"Thank you," sniffled Miss Rabbit.

"When did all this happen?" I asked.

"Probably between 8:00 and 10:00 this morning."

"Any guess who might have done this?" I

probed. I noticed Miss Rabbit was wiping frosting off of her pajamas, whiskers, and nose. She clearly hadn't had time for her morning bath.

"No!" wailed Miss Rabbit. "I don't have a crumb of an idea!"

The captain pointed to the window. In the distance, Fowler the Owl was reading the newspaper in her maple tree. Everyone on the farm knew that Fowler liked rabbits. She liked them for breakfast. She liked them for lunch. And she loved them for dinner.

"Does Fowler come around here?" I asked.

"No, she won't mess with me. I have a black belt in karate!" said Miss Rabbit with a quick chop of her hind legs.

"And ma'am, whom did you invite to the party?"

"Porcini and Hot Dog. You don't think either of them is the thief, do you?"

"Too soon to tell." I snapped shut the cover of my notepad.

The captain checked the door. I checked the windows. There was no sign of a break-in. Could it be an inside job?

"Does anyone have a key to your rabbit hole?" I asked.

Miss Rabbit shook her head, sending crumbs and frosting flying.

"One last question. Where were you when the cake was taken?"

"I was taking a quick catnap."

Hmm . . .a catnap. Such an odd thing for a bunny to do.

I taped off the crime scene. The captain dusted for prints and took photos. This case was going to be a hard nut to crack. A hard nut indeed.

Suspects and Clues

Suspect #1

11:00 am, Fowler's Maple Tree

"Hoo-hoo," said Fowler, peeking her head out of her hole. "What brings you two tasty treats to my tree?"

"Investigating a case," I said, holding up my badge. "Detective Wilcox and Captain Griswold, MFIs. Where were you between 8:00 and 10:00 this morning?"

"I was chasing a field mouse."

"Do you have any witnesses?" If someone had seen her, she'd have an alibi.

"There was one, but I ate him."

The captain shot her his "don't-mess-with-this-mouse" look. I shot her mine.

"You know it's 30 years behind bars if you eat an officer on this farm," I warned. "You don't want to be a jailbird now, do you?"

"Of course not! Besides, I like my meals tender. Everyone knows MFIs are too hard-boiled to make good eats."

I chose to ignore that last comment. The captain glared at her with his "I'll-show-you-who's-hard-boiled" look.

"Your tree faces Miss Rabbit's hole. Have you seen anyone come or go from Miss Rabbit's in the last four hours?"

"Just Miss Rabbit and the two of you. What's this all about anyway?" asked Fowler.

"A cake," I said.

"A rabbit cake?" asked Fowler. "I love rabbit cake, especially with mouse frosting."

I scowled. "No, a carrot cake."

"I don't know anything about a missing carrot cake." Fowler fluffed up her feathers, all innocent-like.

"I didn't say it was missing."

"You wouldn't be here if it were found," said Fowler.

"Tell us what you know." I pulled out my trusty notepad again. "Or if you prefer, we can finish this talk down at the station."

Fowler frowned, but she gave me the scoop. "Miss Rabbit baked a cake all right. A carrot cake, like you said. I could smell that awful thing all the way up here. And then she took a walk in her pajamas."

"In her pajamas?" I asked. "That's odd. Where did she go?"

"Toward Porcini's. Look, I'm not a tattle-telling parrot, but if you ask me, that sneaky porker, Porcini, is your thief. He could sniff out a breadcrumb on the moon. And he'll eat anything, too. Even vegetables!"

"Thanks for the tip." I pocketed my notepad. "And don't fly out of town any time soon."

The captain and I rushed to the squad car. Next stop, Porcini's.

Frankly, this case was moving slower than molasses. Slower than molasses indeed.

11:45 am, Porcini's Pigpen

"Hey, Porcini!" I yelled, as we arrived at the pen. "Detective Wilcox and Captain Griswold here, MFIs, on a case."

The captain waved his badge in front of Porcini's snout.

"What were you doing between 8:00 and 10:00 this morning?" I asked.

"I was resting up between meals, like I always do, when Miss Rabbit stopped by."

Porcini snuffled around the squad car. He must have smelled the cheese donuts!

The captain pushed the pig away and flashed him one of his toughest glares.

"When was this exactly?" I asked.

"I'm not sure, maybe around 9:00." Porcini waddled back to his sty, slurping up banana peels on his way.

"And what did she want?"

"Strangely enough, she didn't say. But she sure was acting like a funny bunny."

"Funny ha ha or funny odd?" I asked.

"She didn't say a word — not even a peep when I asked if she wanted a nice hot cup of slop! And she was still wearing her pajamas. So I walked her back home, like the polite pig I am."

"And is that when you took the cake?" I asked.

Porcini's cheeks turned the color of a red hot chili pepper.

"I may take the cake as the best corn thief in town, but sirs, I am not a common cake thief! Oink!"

The captain handed me Porcini's rap sheet. (That's a record of arrests for all you non-cops.) It was a mile long for corn robberies, but he had no cake priors.

"Seems like you've spent some time in the pen," I said, hoping his reaction would give me a clue.

"Why peck at the past? I did my time and now I'm clean. I bet Hot Dog ate the cake.

That slobbering hound has a sweet tooth."

"That sounds like the pot calling the kettle black. Mind if we have a look around?"

"Go right ahead! I have nothing to hide."

The captain and I waded through Porcini's muddy pen.

"What a pigsty!" I said. "We'll never find anything here."

The captain twitched his whiskers and nodded.

"Let's hope Hot Dog has some answers," I said. "And that his place isn't as stinky!"

Truth to tell, this case was inching along slower than ketchup out of a bottle. Much slower indeed.

12:00 pm, Dirt Road Leading to Hot Dog's House

"Captain, stop the car!" I shouted. "There's something up ahead. It's orange."

The captain grabbed his magnifying glass and tweezers. He picked up the object.

"A carrot!" I said.

I ran back to the squad car to get the crime scene photos.

"This carrot matches the ones we found in Miss Rabbit's kitchen. We're onto something."

The captain twitched his tail furiously. He pointed.

"Another carrot." I picked it up. And right by the front door, the captain found two more.

"Looks like Hot Dog's got himself in a bit of a pickle," I said. "A pickle indeed."

12:05 pm, Dog House

Knock. Knock. The captain rapped on the door.

"Open up! MFIs!" I called out.

The door opened slowly. I shouldered my way in.

"Detective Wilcox and Captain Griswold here!" I announced. "Is that carrot cake I smell?"

"I don't smell anything," said Hot Dog.

For a dog, that was a pretty incredible claim. He was surprisingly cool as a cucumber.

The captain tapped me on the shoulder. He pointed to the flour, eggs, milk, vanilla, carrots, and dog biscuits on the kitchen table.

"What's all this?" I asked.

"Breakfast."

"Looks like cake ingredients to me," I said. "If you don't spill the beans now, we're going to finish this talk down at the station."

The captain flashed his "you're-in-hot-water-now" look.

"All right, I admit it! I baked a cake, but I didn't take the cake!" Hot Dog insisted.

"What do you mean? Give us the facts and just the facts." I pulled out my notepad.

"I did go over to Miss Rabbit's, but only to see if she needed help setting up for her party."

"What happened?" I grilled him.

"I knocked on the door. Nobody answered. So I peeked in the window. And that's when I saw cake crumbs, carrots, and frosting EVERY-WHERE — on the table, on the floor, and all over Miss Rabbit's bathrobe, which was right in the middle of the mess!"

Now that I thought about it, I'd expect an apron, not a bathrobe.

"And then what happened?" I started taking notes.

"I heard someone coming. I panicked and ran home."

The captain made his "that's-the-fishiest-story-I-ever-heard" face.

"Woof's honor!" Hot Dog protested. "I felt so bad that Miss Rabbit's cake was gone, I decided to bake her another one."

"Captain, dollars to donuts, he's telling the truth. Look at

these prints from the crime scene. The thief has small, narrow feet. Hot Dog's paws are big and wide. He couldn't be the thief."

With no more suspects, this investigation was scraping the bottom of the apple barrel. Think. Think. Think. The captain and I started to pace. One, two, three steps forward. One, two, three steps back.

I grabbed a donut from my pocket. Cheese donuts always helped me think. And sure enough, that's when it hit me.

"Holy cannoli, Captain! I've got a plan. Hot Dog, we'll need your cake. With some luck, maybe we'll catch our thief red-handed. Or frosting-handed as the case may be!"

Chapter 4

Video Surveillance
and Stakeout

12:30 pm, Fowler's Maple Tree

We set up two video surveillance cameras. One on top of Fowler's tree, facing Miss Rabbit's front door, and another inside Miss Rabbit's kitchen, facing Hot Dog's cake.

Then we waited.

And waited.

And waited.

The smell of carrot cake drifted across the farm, past Fowler's maple tree, Porcini's pen, and Hot Dog's house.

"Pee-ew!" Fowler hooted.

"Fowler is clearly not our thief," I whispered to the captain. Just then Porcini and Hot Dog showed up like two peas in a pod.

"Any luck with the investigation?" asked Hot Dog.

"Would they be sitting here if they had the thief?" shouted Fowler from the tree above.

"Whoever the thief is, he's very good," Porcini observed.

"Or she!" cried Fowler.

The captain looked at his watch. Tick.
Tock. Tick. Tock. Two hours had gone by. Nothing.
Three hours, four hours, five hours. Still nothing.
The clock kept ticking. Day turned to night and
night to day. Porcini, Hot Dog, the captain, and
I were packed in like sardines as we fell asleep
at the base of Fowler's tree. Everybody snored.
Everybody's stomach rumbled. Nothing else
happened.

I was beginning to think maybe our goose
was cooked. Cooked well done indeed.

The Morning Starts
with a Scream

9:00 am, Home of Miss Rabbit

"Help!" cried Miss Rabbit. "The cake is gone!"

"Holy guacamole! Miss Rabbit's in trouble!" I shouted.

We all rushed over and slid down the rabbit hole. Cake crumbs, carrots, and frosting were EVERYWHERE — on the floor, on the table, and all over Miss Rabbit.

"Are you all right?" I asked.

"Yes," sniffled Miss Rabbit.

"Did you see the thief?" I asked.

She shook her head, flinging out crumbs. Porcini hurried over to lick them up.

The captain pointed to the video camera.

"Good thing we have the two videotapes!"
I said.

Fowler brought down the tape from her
tree and we watched it first. It showed Porcini,
Hot Dog, the captain, and me all rushing into
the house.

"Where's the thief?" asked Miss Rabbit,
wiping cream cheese off of her pajamas, whiskers,
and nose.

"Maybe there's a problem with this camera," I
said. "Let's look at the second video. Miss Rabbit,
you may want to sit down."

The room was silent.

"There's nothing on this tape," cried Miss Rabbit.

"Patience. It's still rolling," I said, when the tape picked up the presence of a shadow.

"I can't watch!" screamed Porcini.

"Me, neither!" cried Hot Dog.

"Who?!" hooted Fowler.

"Quiet!" I shouted.

The captain shot everyone his "or else!" look.

And then the blurry image of a figure appeared.

"Is it over?" screamed Porcini.
"I'm scared!" cried Hot Dog.
"Who?!" hooted Fowler.
"Shush!" I shouted.
The captain glared his "be quiet!" look.

The figure slowly came into focus.

The pajamas.

The whiskers.

The nose.

And the ears.

"Miss Rabbit!" cried everyone.

"No!" Miss Rabbit wailed. "That can't be right. I was asleep."

"You were sleepwalking," I explained.

"And great corn dogs! Sleep eating, too!" squealed Porcini. "Why didn't I think of that, eating all day AND all night? What could be better?"

"I'm sorry for all the trouble I caused." Miss Rabbit was beet red from embarrassment.

"No problem," I assured her. "That's what we're here for."

"And I guess I'll have to cancel my party. Since there's no cake."

"Actually, there is a cake," said Hot Dog. "I never bake just one."

Chapter 6

The Long-Awaited Party

4:00 pm, Home of Miss Rabbit

"Having all my friends gathered together is the icing on the cake!" said Miss Rabbit. "Detectives, many thanks for your hard work."

"Our pleasure! This case was a piece of cake after all!" I put away my notepad.

The captain smiled his "easy-as-pie" face.

"Hot Dog, thank you for your beautiful cake!" Miss Rabbit gushed.

"Any time!" said Hot Dog, giving Miss Rabbit a hug. "Now let's eat! I'm hungry as a wolf!"

"Two wolves!" agreed Porcini.

Miss Rabbit nibbled a piece. "My, this cake is crunchy!"

"Crunchy indeed!" I said.

"Crunchier and tastier than it smells," hooted Fowler.

The captain chomped so loudly, he was speechless.

Porcini finished one slice and started on another.

"Is carrot cake always so crunchy?" I asked.

"It's my secret ingredient. Dog biscuits. Do you like it?" asked Hot Dog.

Everyone stopped eating except Porcini and Hot Dog. They finished every last crumb.

"DEEEE-LICIOUS!" pronounced Porcini.

"Now that's how you make a cake disappear!" Hot Dog smiled.

5:00 pm, Case Closed.

Boys and girls, the case you've just read was about thieves on Ed's farm.

Every day food goes missing from the farm. Sometimes it's lost. Sometimes it's stolen. Sometimes it just runs away.

With all these animals, you can be sure of one thing: trouble is sure to hatch. These are the cases for MFIs.

Whatever the food, whatever the crime, MFIs make the bad guys do the time.

Mollie Katzen's Carrot Cake

This is an easy cake that is very moist.

You can have fun grating a peeled, fat carrot on a hand grater for this, if you're careful to watch your knuckles. You can also have someone help you safely grate a carrot with a food processor (grating attachment) or simply buy carrots already grated.

You will need four bowls for this. Make sure they are big enough so you can enjoy mixing without worrying about spills. Unwrap the butter up to an hour ahead of time and place it directly in the bowl to soften.

- Nonstick cooking spray
- ½ cup (1 stick) butter, softened in a big bowl
- 1 cup (packed) light brown sugar
- 2 large eggs
- 1 teaspoon pure vanilla extract
- 1 ½ cups all-purpose flour
- ¼ teaspoon salt
- 1 teaspoon baking powder
- ¼ teaspoon baking soda
- 1 teaspoon cinnamon
- 1 ½ cups (packed) grated carrot
- 6 tablespoons buttermilk

1) Preheat the oven to 350°F (or 325°F, if using a glass pan) and spray a 6 X 9-inch baking pan (or its equivalent) with nonstick spray.

2) Begin beating the butter with an electric hand mixer on medium speed. After about a minute, sprinkle in the sugar and beat at medium speed again, until the sugar is all mixed in.

3) Break one egg into a bowl and slide it into the butter bowl. Beat again until it's mixed in, then do the same with the second egg. When it's combined, add the vanilla and beat at high speed for about 2 minutes or until very fluffy. Use a rubber spatula to scrape the sides of the bowl a few times, so you can include all the bits.

4) Measure the flour and other dry ingredients into the third bowl and mix slowly by hand for just a few seconds until all combined.

5) Combine the carrot and buttermilk in the fourth bowl and stir to completely combine.

6) Add about 1/3 of the flour mixture to the butter-sugar mixture, stirring with a spoon until it is pretty much mixed in. Then add about half the carrot mixture and mix that in too. (No beating necessary at this point, just spoon-mixing.)

7) Stir in another 1/3 of the flour, followed by the rest of the carrot mixture, followed by the remaining flour, mixing after each addition. You can use a rubber spatula, in addition to the spoon, to scrape the sides of the bowl.

8) Transfer the batter to the prepared pan, spreading the mixture evenly into place. Bake in the center of the oven for 25 to 35 minutes or until the top is springy to the touch (careful!) and the edges are lightly golden. Carefully remove from the oven and cool completely before cutting into squares and enjoying.

Makes 8 to 10 servings.

Cooking and baking demand careful attention. Neither the author nor publisher assumes responsibility for any accident, misadventure, or over-eating from the use of this recipe.

Heartfelt thanks from RN (alias: Snack Snatcher) to special agents Liza Fleissig and Ginger Harris-Dontzin, for their endless support and encouragement.

EVIDENCE